To the Rescue!

by
Debbi Chocolate

NEATE™ Series – Created by Wade Hudson

FICTION

Just Us Books, Inc.
East Orange, New Jersey

Published by
Just Us Books, Inc.
356 Glenwood Avenue
East Orange, NJ 07017

NEATE™ was created by Wade Hudson and is a trademark of Just Us Books, Inc. All of the characters in this book are fictitious, and any resemblance to actual persons, living or dead, is purely coincidental.

Cover art copyright 1992 by Melodye Rosales

NEATE™ To the Rescue copyright © 1992 by Debbi Chocolate, published by
Just Us Books, Inc. All rights reserved.
ISBN: 0-940975-42-4 Library of Congress Number 92-72004
Printed in Canada

12 11 10 9 8 7 6 5 4 3 2

For Michael Chocolate
1954 – 1992
and
For Ora Mae Chocolate

With Love,
DC

CHAPTER ONE

B-b-brrriing!! **B-b-brrriing!!**

It was the alarm clock. Naimah Jackson peeked from beneath a blanket and a bundle of clothes piled on her bed. She had fallen asleep on the very spot she had sorted her laundry the night before.

Bright sunlight flooded the room causing Naimah to squint and burrow beneath the clothes and the blanket where it was dark and warm.

B-b-brrriing!! B-b-brrriing!!

Naimah tried to ignore the clock, but the sound wouldn't let her sleep. Finally, she dragged herself out of bed and flung clothing everywhere in search of the annoying clock.

As she glanced around her bedroom she caught a reflection of herself in the mirror. Naimah was brown-skinned, slender, and neighbors said she was the spitting image of her mother. A self-assured thirteen year old, she was in the eighth grade at DuSable Junior High School.

Naimah looked everywhere for the clock but couldn't find it. It should have been on the night stand.

"Where are you clock?" she muttered.

Naimah stood in the middle of her room, which now looked like a disaster area. Not only was dirty laundry scattered about, a pair of mismatched socks hung haphazardly over her vanity mirror. Books tumbled from her school bag and a stash of rap magazines was strewn across her bedroom floor. Naimah scratched her head sleepily. She didn't want the ringing to wake the whole house—especially Rodney, the eight-year-old human pest—and her brother.

Rodney wasn't really a bad brother. He was more like a gnat that kept buzzing around your head.

Naimah picked up the latest issue of *Young Sisters and Brothers* magazine from the floor and placed it on the night stand. Then she renewed her search for the clock. Why wasn't it on the night stand where it was supposed to be?

B-b-brrriing!! B-b-brrrriing!!

The irritating sound was beginning to give her a headache. Naimah saw another magazine laying at the foot of her bed.

"Where did this come from?" she whispered as she reached down and picked up the magazine. It was a *Brotherman* comic book.

"This belongs to the pest," she said out loud. Suddenly, Naimah heard her mother's voice calling from the bedroom next to her own.

"Naimah? Naimah? What's the matter with you, girl?! This is Saturday! Turn off that alarm clock!" Naimah's mother didn't sound mad, but she didn't sound happy, either.

Naimah sighed and looked towards the door. There he was! The human pest stood in the doorway chuckling. His hands were cupped over his mouth to muffle the sound.

He's probably been standing there the entire time watching me make a fool of myself, Naimah thought.

"Why you little..." Naimah hissed. "You set my alarm clock and hid it, didn't you?" Before Rodney could answer, Naimah grabbed a pillow from the bed and threw it at him. Rodney threw the pillow back at her. A furious pillow fight had begun.

B-b-brrriing!! B-b-brrriing!!

Through all of the commotion the annoying sound of the alarm clock never missed a ring.

"*Naimah Zakia Jackson!*" Now Naimah's mom was standing in the doorway, her hands placed firmly on her hips.

"Now I know you two know better. . . *especially* you, Naimah!"

Suddenly, the clock stopped alarming. For a moment everything was quiet.

"But Mama," Naimah protested, "Rodney started it. He hid the clock."

"No I didn't," Rodney countered.

"Yes you did!"

"Prove it!"

Naimah held up Rodney's *Brotherman* comic book.

"Is this proof enough?" she snapped.

"Hush! Both of you," warned Ms. Gordon. She took one look around the room, crossed her arms, and turned to her children.

"Naimah," she ordered, you get downstairs and help me get breakfast started. After breakfast, I want this room cleaned. Rodney, I want your room cleaned, too."

Shannon Gordon spoke in her "no nonsense" voice. A community leader and a member of the city council, sometimes Ms. Gordon sounded as if she were in council chambers addressing an important issue.

"That's no fair, Mama," groaned Rodney.

Ms. Gordon didn't say a word. She put her hands on her hips again and gave her son a look that said she was very serious.

Just then, Naimah remembered the referendum. Her mother's "no nonsense" voice had reminded her. For the past few weeks Naimah had been busy helping her mother campaign for a new ward map.

Several members of the city council wanted to change the city wards. Although they denied it, their main intention was to take away some of the voting power minorities had gained over the last few years. They were led by David Russell, who was once a member of the council. Naimah's mother had defeated him in the last two elections. But it had been David Russell's idea to change the wards. Until 10 years ago, Russell had worked as a policeman in the third ward, in which he was now running for office. During that time, Russell had had several run-ins with community leaders, including Shannon Gordon, over his mistreatment of the residents that he was sworn to serve and protect. Russell made it clear in his campaign speeches that he felt African Americans were trying to take over the city.

Ms. Gordon represented the third ward, which was predominantly African American. The new map, proposed by Russell, would add a number of predominantly white suburbs to the third ward. Because most of the people who lived in those suburbs were white, Russell felt he would get their votes and the council seat. He planted fear in the minds of white voters by telling them that a vote for Shannon Gordon's plan was a vote supporting an African-American takeover of the city council. Ms. Gordon had proposed a plan she felt would be fair to all citizens. It was up to the voters to decide which plan they preferred.

For weeks David Russell had conducted a vicious campaign to help his plan win. No one was sure how the vote would go. Naimah had stayed up late the night before watching the returns but none of the television stations could predict the winning plan. Around midnight, Naimah had fallen asleep.

Naimah knew how much the result meant to her mother's career. The city election was just two weeks away and if Russell's referendum plan won, it could be very difficult for Ms. Gordon to win her council seat again.

Naimah looked at her mother. Like Naimah, Shannon Gordon was tall and slender. She always wore trim, tailored clothes and she was *never* seen in public without wearing a hat to embellish her outfit. Fedoras and panamas that could only be described as eye-catching, colorful, and flamboyant were her favorites.

Some people said Shannon Gordon and her

daughter looked so much alike they could pass for sisters. By nature, Ms. Gordon was a fighter. She had helped many people in the city while serving on the city council and those people respected and loved her. But this morning Ms. Gordon had a worried look on her face.

"Mama, did we win?" Naimah asked softly. She could sense something was wrong.

"No, honey, we didn't," answered Ms. Gordon. Naimah could see the sadness in her face. Naimah felt sad, too.

"What are you going to do?!"

"I'm going to fight back like I always do!" Ms. Gordon replied. She turned and walked purposefully out of the room. Naimah quickly followed her mother downstairs. The mean trick Rodney had played with the alarm clock didn't seem so important, now.

CHAPTER TWO

Downstairs in the kitchen, Naimah poured herself a tall glass of cold orange juice while her mother mixed the pancake batter. The coffee was perking on the stove and Naimah breathed in the warm, delicious smell. As she set the table she thought about last night's vote. Suddenly, there was a thump at the kitchen door. Naimah pulled back the curtain and saw Anthony on his bicycle delivering the morning paper. Anthony Young was her neighbor and classmate.

Naimah ran to the door and called out to him. Anthony's shoulders sagged a little under the weight of the newspaper bag he carried. He was short, medium-brown skinned, and wore glasses. Anthony was really sensitive about his height and people who didn't know him well usually thought he was shy. But Naimah knew better. Anthony just took time to think things through. What stood out most about Anthony was that he was always neatly dressed. Today, Anthony wore khaki pants, a green cardigan sweater, and loafers.

Anthony lived next door with his mother, Patricia Young. He didn't have any brothers or sisters, and he'd never known his father.

The two families lived on Mary Street, which was lined with red, yellow, and brown brick bungalows. The nice thing about their street was that the neighbors seemed as familiar and as friendly as the houses. In fact, the neighbors were more like family than friends. Just about everyone in the neighborhood had helped campaign for the redistricting plan that Shannon Gordon had proposed. Naimah's closest friends had helped, too. Tayesha Williams, Eddie Delaney, Elizabeth Butler, and Anthony all attended DuSable Junior High.

Anthony, his bag of newspapers, and his bike now stood at Naimah's kitchen door.

"You heard about the vote?" Naimah asked Anthony.

"Yeah, I heard early this morning," Anthony answered. He swung his bike around and started to push off.

"You could at least stop long enough to say, 'I'm sorry!'" Naimah yelled at him.

Anthony looked back and waved to his friend. He pulled his bike up wheely-style and shouted over his shoulder, "Talk to you later!"

Naimah waved the paper at him and as soon as he rode out of sight she unrolled it carefully. When she saw the front page her mouth dropped wide open.

Staring back at her from page one was a picture of David Russell with a big grin plastered all over his face. Russell's arms were folded and his chest stuck out like an over-stuffed Thanksgiving Day turkey.

David Russell looked just as cocky and conceited as ever. He posed as though he had just been elected mayor of the city. Beneath the photograph the caption explained:

RUSSELL'S PLAN WINS:
CITY WARDS TO UNDERGO
MAJOR RESTRUCTURING

Another headline read:

WHAT ARE GORDON'S
CHANCES OF RE-ELECTION?

Naimah refolded the paper and closed the door.

When the family finally sat down to breakfast, Naimah noticed that her mother had not eaten a bite. Mr. Gordon was trying to be supportive.

Naimah wasn't hungry either.

"Look, honey," said Mr. Gordon to his wife, "this is only a minor setback."

While her dad tried to comfort her mom, Naimah started clearing the dishes from the breakfast table. When she neared her mother's plate, she put the dishes down and gave her mom a hug. Mr. Gordon smiled and winked at Naimah.

Rodney Gordon, Senior was Naimah's stepdad and Rodney, Junior's father. But it was times like this that Naimah loved her stepfather just as much as she loved her own dad, who had died when she was three years old.

"Do you want me to warm your food, Mom?" Naimah offered.

"No, thank you, honey," her mother answered. "I know this is only a minor setback, but my stomach is too tied up in knots right now to even think about food."

"I'll take it," piped Rodney. And then, in one swift stroke, Rodney scooped the pile of pancakes from his mother's plate onto his own. He was like a pilot diving to bomb an enemy target.

"Where did you ever learn to be so gross?" Naimah smirked.

"From you, brainless," Rodney shot back at his sister.

"Hey, cut it out you two," Mr. Gordon jumped in. "Don't you realize what has just happened?!"

"Sorry," Naimah apologized.

"Me too," Rodney chimed in.

Naimah bent over her mother's shoulders and studied the front page of the paper now spread out on the kitchen table.

"Mom, I just can't understand why your plan didn't win," she said dejectedly. "It should have won!"

Ms. Gordon sighed. "The people who supported it didn't come out and vote like they should have. That's always the case. If you don't fight for what you believe in until the end, you can't expect to win."

"We can go to court," Mr. Gordon said angrily.

"We'll have to look at a lot of options," Ms. Gordon said. "You know, my seat isn't the only one that's in jeopardy. This city might lose over half of the African-American members of the city council. Russell's plan could undo years of progress that people have been fighting so hard for."

Ms. Gordon tapped her index finger on the newspaper dishearteningly.

Naimah's ears began to burn and the tears were swelling in her eyes. "You have to fight back, Mom!" she said. "You *have* to!"

"I plan to fight back, Naimah—bright and early Monday morning."

"Mama, don't you get it? The only way to fight someone like David Russell is to use the same ammunition he uses."

"I think Naimah's right for once," agreed Rodney. "I can think of a million ways to fix that old scuzzball. At least a million."

"Now you two just hold it right there," countered Ms. Gordon. There was a firmness in her voice this time, along with that look that could stop a steam engine.

"You guys *listen*. Monday morning, your dad and I will meet with other concerned people so that we can decide what to do. I have no intentions of fighting David Russell on his level. I don't ever want to stoop to the dirty tricks and tactics he uses to try to win an election. So until tomorrow, let's just relax. Okay? Is that clear?" Ms. Gordon looked around the table.

"Okay, *okay*," conceded Rodney, stuffing the last sausage into his mouth. But it was only with reluctance that his sister relented. Naimah was already making plans to take her own actions to help her mother's bid for re-election. She could hardly wait to meet with Anthony, Elizabeth, Eddie, and Tayesha.

She knew she could always count on them.

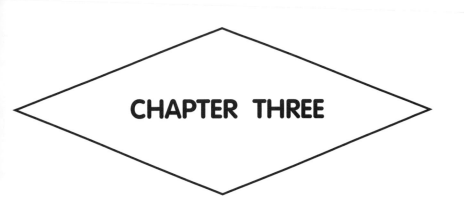

CHAPTER THREE

Monday
October 18th

Dear Mr. & Ms. Delaney:

I worked with Eddie on his geometry today, and I gave him some extra-credit work to do. He seems to understand the problems a little better now, and needs to bring an isosceles triangle to class tomorrow. His behavior has also improved, except for his tendency to doodle on his desk.

Ms. Renfrow

"Except for doodling on his desk?" Mr. Delaney frowned. The Delaneys had just finished eating dinner. Eddie Delaney was licking the remnants of tapioca pudding from his spoon when his father opened the letter he had brought home from school that afternoon. Eddie wouldn't look up at his father. Instead, he continued to scrape his spoon around the empty dessert dish. The noise had finally begun to irritate his mother. Juanita Delaney gently pried the spoon loose from her son's slender hand.

"Doodling on his desk?" repeated Mr. Delaney. He looked from the letter to his son and back to the letter again.

"What *is* the matter with you, boy?"

Eddie finally looked up, he still didn't say anything, but he had a really weird look on his face.

"Now look, Eddie," began his dad, "I have told you time and time again that school is where you go to get an education. Doodling on your desk is not what your mother and I send you to school for."

Eddie sighed deeply. Here it comes, he thought.

"When I was in school, I was like your sister. I was ambitious. I wanted to be somebody. And I studied hard so I could make my parents proud."

Eddie picked up a slice of bread and started to paint it with butter. He was sorry now that he had been so stupid. Why did he write all over his school desk? And why did he get caught? Eddie sighed quietly.

"Your father and I have high hopes for you, Eddie," said Ms. Delaney softly. "For you *and* your sister."

Eddie took a bite from the buttered bread. Then he poured himself a glass of milk and drank it all down in several gulps.

"After all," smiled Juanita Delaney, "We didn't name you after Dr. Martin Luther King, Jr. for no reason."

Gee thanks for the pressure, Mom, thought Eddie.

Eddie's given name was Martin Edward Delaney, but everyone called him Eddie. He preferred it that way. His sister Daisey was named after Daisey Bates, who was also a civil rights leader.

"You need to become more responsible, like your sister," said Mr. Delaney. Eddie's sister was a sophomore at Spelman College and every semester she managed to make the Dean's List. How could anyone measure up to her? Mr. Delaney looked at his watch. He had a Mason's meeting to attend and Eddie was counting the minutes. He knew this lecture wouldn't last much longer.

"I made it, son. Your mother made it."

Great dad, thought Eddie. He stuffed another bite of bread into his mouth. I'm glad you made it. The next question is—are you going to make your meeting?

"Yes," Mr. Delaney went on, "I studied hard. And I played hard, too. But most important, when I was in school I seized the opportunities."

"You'd better be going, Floyd," Ms. Delaney interrupted. "You'll be late for your lodge meeting."

"I'm ready," Mr. Delaney said. Then he turned to face Eddie. "I hate to do it son, but if I don't see some improvement I'm going to have to ground you for the rest of the marking period." Eddie groaned and slid down in his seat.

"I *mean* that," his father emphasized.

Mr. Delaney walked out of the door. Eddie remained in his chair at the table until he heard the car pull out of the driveway.

Finally! he thought. He glanced quickly at the clock on the wall. It was nearly quarter to seven, almost time for Naimah's meeting.

Anthony Young had just hung his empty newspaper bag over the handles of his bicycle. It was a regular routine. Every night, after he finished his homework, Anthony got everything ready for the next day. He would put his school clothes out on the chair in his room. Then he would take the newspaper bag to the garage and hang it over his bicycle so that in the morning he wouldn't waste time looking for it. Anthony had had the same newspaper route for three years. And in those three years he had never missed a delivery day. He came in from the garage and walked into the kitchen.

"Need any help with the dishes, Mom?"

"I don't think so, honey," answered his mother. "But you can keep me company."

Anthony pulled up a chair and sat down at the kitchen table. He was amazed at how his mother was able to work, come home every night and cook, and still help him with his homework.

Pat Young worked for the *Daily World*, where she had started six years ago as a typist. Now she was a manager for the classified ads department. Anthony was proud of his mother. She had come a long way on very little. But, sometimes he found himself wishing there was a man in their lives. Someone he could look up to, like Eddie's father. Anthony admired Mr. Delaney so much that he dreamed of becoming a lawyer one day just like him. Anthony felt he was the man of the house. It was up to him, he thought, to look after his mother. But actually, Patricia Young was capable of taking care of herself and Anthony. And she had proved it.

"What are you thinking about, man? Ms. Young asked her son.

"Nothing."

They were quiet for a moment.

"Mom," said Anthony thoughtfully, "What do you think are Ms. Gordon's chances of keeping her city council seat?"

"It will be very tough. The voters from the suburban wards are new to our ways and needs. I'm afraid most of them may not vote for an African-American candidate. They haven't done so in past elections. But who knows? Anything can happen in politics."

"Yeah, maybe so," said Anthony getting up from the kitchen table. "Mom, I'm going over to Elizabeth's for awhile if it's okay."

"Okay," said Ms. Young. But don't stay too late."

"I won't," Anthony called over his shoulder.

Naimah knocked on the door to Liz's house. No one answered. She knocked again. Finally Liz's mother opened the door.

"Hi, Ms. Butler."

"Hello, Naimah. Come on in. Elizabeth's upstairs in her bedroom trying on some new and ridiculous outfit she just bought." Ms. Butler shook her head. Naimah liked the way Ms. Butler kept cool about Liz's wild clothes and hairdos, even though she didn't approve.

"Go right on up," she said to Naimah. "It's the party room with all the noise floating out from beneath the door."

Naimah laughed and bounded two steps at a time up the carpeted stairs. At the top of the stairs she bumped into Angela, Liz's four-year-old sister.

"Hi, Angie," said Naimah, almost out of breath. Angie was pulling a plastic, musical, air bubble filled with colored balls that popped and jumped when the toy rolled across the floor.

"Hi, Nima," said Angie brightly. She couldn't pronounce Naimah's name too well.

"What 'cha got?" asked Naimah.

"Popcorn machine."

"It's pretty. Where's Liz?"

"In there," answered Angie, pointing to her big sister's room, "making too much noise." Naimah smiled and Angie walked slowly down the hallway, pulling her toy behind her.

Just then, Sandra, Liz's older sister, walked out of the bathroom. Sandy was a sophomore at Roosevelt High. Naimah thought Sandy was so cool. Sandy wore her hair in long dredlocks. Sandy had a quick smile and deep dimples.

"Hi, Nima," said Sandy, imitating her little sister.

"Hi, Sandy," Naimah replied, smiling.

"How's the junior high posse?" Sandy was always teasing Naimah, Liz, and Tayesha about catching up with her high school crowd.

"Only one more year," answered Naimah good naturedly.

"If you're looking for Miss Teen Talent Search," said Sandy, pointing to Liz's room, "just follow all the noise." Sandy strolled into her own room and closed the door.

The vibrations from a thumping rap song rattled the door that led to Liz's room. Naimah knocked first and then opened the door. The music was so loud that Liz didn't hear Naimah come in.

Elizabeth was dressed in a black spandex body suit, red leather ankle boots, and she had a red silk scarf tied around her neck. She was dancing in front of the mirror.

Liz was a dark, attractive girl and she wore her hair in braids that fell to her shoulders. The song thumping on her CD player was from a Queen Latifah disc. Liz was also playing a Queen Latifah music video on her television with the sound turned down. Queen Latifah was one of her favorite performers.

"Liz!" shouted Naimah. Liz turned around and saw her friend standing at the door.

"*Heeeyyyy!*" she tried to yell over the music before walking over to the stereo and turning down the volume on the CD player. "Come on in."

Naimah plopped down on Liz's water bed. She loved to visit Liz. Everything about Liz was a fashion statement. The walls of her room were covered with travel posters of Hawaii, St. Croix, and Trinidad. And Liz was the only kid Naimah knew who actually had her own water bed. Of course her father bought it for her. He bought her everything.

"Girl," said Liz excitedly. "I really feel up for this Rawley talent search."

"You think you might win the color television? The gift certificates?" Naimah whispered wide-eyed.

"Might win?!" I can feel it, girl!"

Liz left the mirror long enough to crawl over the water bed to get to the other side of the room. Naimah laid there perfectly still and enjoyed the gentle bouncing waves.

"It's all happening so fast," Liz exclaimed. "It seems like yesterday that Ms. Lewis called my mom and dad about the contest...a national contest at that. I can't remember when I've been this excited.

"My mom's not too ecstatic about my being in the contest. But my dad said to go for it. He bought the suit and boots for the audition. Liz pointed to a sparkling, sequined outfit on the foot of the bed.

Naimah held the outfit up. "That's *baaad*, girl! You'll knock 'em dead in this." Naimah gave her friend a quick hug.

"Thanks, girlfriend," Liz said, smiling at Naimah. "That means a lot coming from you."

Naimah looked at her watch. "Where is everybody? It's almost seven o'clock."

Tayesha Williams had just finished washing the dishes when the telephone rang.

"Tayesha, telephone," called Ms. Williams.

"Thanks, Mom." Tayesha wiped her hands dry on a dish towel and picked up the telephone receiver from the kitchen wall.

"Hello?"

"Tayesha? Liz. Are you coming to the meeting or not?"

"I'm just finishing the dishes," Tayesha answered. "I'll be there in a few minutes."

She hung up the telephone. "Mom, I'm going next door to study with Liz and Naimah."

"What time is it?"

"Almost seven o'clock."

"Tayesha, you know your father and I don't like you to go out after dark on a school night." There was a moment of silence.

"Did you finish washing the dishes?"

"Yes." Tayesha's mother was now standing in the kitchen. Ms. Williams was from Germany. She had short, blonde hair and clear blue eyes.

"What about your homework, Tayesha?"

This time it was her father's deep voice. Tayesha could hear him as he made his way up the basement steps. Those heavy boots he wore sure made a lot of noise. Henry Williams was a light-skinned African-American. He was tall, well-built, and wore a thick moustache. He had worked in factories most of his life but now he was a foreman. Mr. Williams was born in Harlem, New York. He didn't have much of a formal education, but he was determined to see that his only child get as much as possible.

He was still wearing his work clothes. He was always repairing something, and tonight was no different. He held a little gadget in his hand.

"Have you finished *all* your homework, little girl?" he asked Tayesha playfully.

"Yes, she's finished," Greta Williams answered for her daughter. "But her bedroom is still a mess."

"Mom," pleaded Tayesha. "Just this once."

"If it's okay with your father, it's okay with me."

"Well, I don't know," her father said, still teasing as he tinkered with the gadget he held in his hands.

"Please, Daddy," begged Tayesha. "Please!"

"Just this once," her father smiled. "But don't be gone too long."

"Thanks, Daddy, I won't." Tayesha rushed out of the house. Greta Williams turned to her husband.

"I just don't want to see her get hurt."

"She'll be all right," Mr. Williams tried to assure his wife. "She'll be fine."

Everyone had finally arrived at Liz's house. Tayesah, Naimah, Eddie, and Anthony.

"This meeting is now called to order," announced Naimah. The five friends were seated around a coffee table on the floor in Liz's basement.

"Okay, guys," Naimah sighed as she pulled a handful of campaign flyers from her book bag. "This is what we're dealing with." She passed the flyers around. "I hope you're looking on an empty stomach."

Liz shrieked when she saw the flyer. Even Liz's shrieks sounded like melodies.

A sketch of Shannon Gordon dressed in army boots, boxer shorts, and an army fatigue jacket covered the flyer. The artist's rendition had Ms. Gordon standing while delivering a speech in the hub of the city council chambers. The council woman's eyes were bulging out of her head and red thread-like veins had been etched meticulously into them.

"Are we going to come up with a plan or are we just going to stand here chilling?" asked a restless Eddie as he frowned at the campaign flyer he held in his hand.

"Relax," chided Anthony. "The old hand-kerchief-head didn't waste anytime, did he?" said Anthony referring to David Russell.

The artist had had a field day with the caricature of the councilwoman. Shannon Gordon's knees and legs were drawn to look like a cartoon. Her hair looked as though it had not seen a comb in weeks.

"How low can you go?" asked Eddie to no one in particular.

"This has got to be the last straw," added Tayesha in disbelief.

"It is," answered Naimah.

"The question is," emphasized Anthony, "what are we going to do about it?"

"How's about toilet-papering his whole lawn for starters," laughed Eddie.

"I don't think so," said Liz as she looked at Naimah. "I think girlfriend's got something more serious on her mind."

"There she goes with that corny *girlfriend* stuff," griped Eddie.

"Buzz off, Eddie!"

"Come on, you guys," Naimah stepped in. "We're here for business. Now, what David Russell needs is a taste of his own medicine." Suddenly, Naimah's eyes lit up like light bulbs. Her mind flashed back to the morning after the referendum and the conversation she'd had with her mother.

". . . because the people who supported it didn't get out and vote like they should have. That's always the case. If you don't fight for what you believe in until the end, you can't expect to win . . ."

"I've got it," said Naimah excitedly. "We can organize our own campaign to get my mother re-elected. Mom's redistricting plan lost because not enough people came out to support it. If enough people had come out to vote we would have won. Don't you see? All we have to do is get more people interested so they will vote. We can do that."

"Hey, that's a good idea," chimed Anthony. "Wouldn't it be a bummer for old handkerchief-head Russell if your mom beat him under his own redistricting plan?"

"That would be neat," added Tayesha. "I can see his face now."

"Yeah, all smashed in from defeat," quipped Eddie.

"But do you think the voters who are new to the district will vote for your mom?" Liz interjected. My dad said your mom will need to get quite a few white votes in order to win—and some Latino votes, too."

"We'll get them," snapped Eddie. "No sweat."

"Elizabeth has a point," Naimah decided. "It won't be that easy to convince white voters to vote for my mom."

Eddie spoke up. "Everybody knows she's the best person for the job," To Eddie, everything always seemed so simple.

Anthony got more and more excited about the idea of working on a campaign of their own. He could barely contain his enthusiasm.

"We can do it, Naimah! I know we can do it! We can make our own campaign flyers and our own posters."

"And whose going to pay for all of that?" It was Eddie again.

"We can all chip in," Tayesha answered. "And we can get donations from other people."

"But we've got to keep it quiet," Naimah warned. "I don't think my mom should know. I think we can do it. But everyone has to be up for a lot of work."

"It's for a good cause," Anthony said.

"I've got a lot of rehearsing to do," Liz said quietly.

"We *all* have things to do," Tayesha jumped in. "Student council election is coming up. Naimah's running for president. And I'm sure the rest of us have important things to do, too. But if we try, we can make time for this campaign."

"I didn't say I wasn't going to help," Liz said defensively. "You know you guys can depend on me."

"Who's running against you for student council president, Naimah?" asked Anthony.

"Pete Russell and Hank Rodriguez," answered Naimah.

"Pete Russell?!" exclaimed Anthony. "David

Russell's kid?" He put his hand on Naimah's shoulder.

"Well, friend, you'll get my vote."

"Mine too," said Tayesha.

"You can count on all of us," added Liz.

"Hey! Not so fast," teased Eddie. "You've got to prove you're worthy of my vote."

"*Booooooooooo*," said Liz, Tayesha, and Anthony in unison.

"This meeting is over," proclaimed Naimah standing up. "Phase one of our very private campaign begins right after school tomorrow." Then she, Liz, Tayesha, and Anthony ushered Eddie up the basement stairs.

CHAPTER FOUR

The next day after school, Naimah sat on the cool marble steps of DuSable Junior High. She could hardly wait for her friends to come out. She had finished a test quickly, so her teacher, Ms. Tillman, had let her out of class early.

It was a bright, windy, autumn afternoon and the falling leaves made a scratching sound as they bounced against the surface of the steps.

Naimah's backpack was bursting at the seams with campaign flyers she'd made for her mother. She'd borrowed ten dollars from her own private savings to get their campaign started. And then, on the way to school, she'd stopped by Hensell's Pharmacy and made almost two hundred copies. Now all she had to do was wait for her posse. Together they would pass out the flyers to the voters of the third ward.

Finally the school bell rang. A wave of students began pouring from the building.

"Yo, Anthony!" shouted Eddie. Naimah spotted Tayesha and Liz who were caught in the current of students. She waved and called out to them. Anthony and Eddie pushed their way towards Naimah and eventually Tayesha and Liz caught up, too.

The two boys greeted each other and gave each other a high five.

"Hey, Naimah," greeted Tayesha and Liz. Naimah opened her backpack and gave each of her friends a stack of campaign flyers.

"The money for these came from my own savings," Naimah explained. "But I'm hoping you guys will be able to pitch in on the next batch."

"No problem," Anthony quickly assured his friend.

"We're with you, Naimah," agreed Tayesha.

Naimah then quickly sketched out a plan for the afternoon. They would all campaign together. First they'd work the West side of Lawndale (which was what the third ward neighborhood was called), and then tomorrow they'd work Lawndale's East side. Thursday they'd work the North side of Lawndale, and then on Friday the South side.

"But mostly African Americans live in Lawndale," Elizabeth pointed out. "What about the new predominantly white neighborhoods that have been added to our ward?"

"Yeah," Eddie agreed. "Elizabeth has a point. But, on the other hand," he seemed to be thinking out loud, "A lot of our own people didn't come out to vote for the referendum. So maybe our own neighborhood is the best place to start campaigning," he decided.

Everyone agreed. The five friends started walking and canvassing their own neighborhood.

Lawndale was predominantly African American but the West side was mixed. Whites, African Americans, Latinos, and Asians lived side by side. As the five teenagers walked through the neighborhood, they passed out flyers to people standing and walking along the streets.

"Vote For Shannon Gordon for City Council."

"Re-elect Shannon Gordon."

Along the way they stopped at barber shops, beauty salons, soul food kitchens, and Vietnamese restaurants. On the corner of Roosevelt and Karlov, the window of the Polish bakery displayed a huge campaign poster of a smiling Shannon Gordon.

"See, I told, you," teased Eddie, pointing to the smiling poster in the bakery shop. "This election's going to be a piece of cake."

It was Elizabeth's idea to turn onto the side streets to hand out flyers to the people living in the houses. The houses in this section of Lawndale were not the quaint, well-kept, red and brown bungalows that lined Mary Street. Instead, they were frame row houses where laundry hung from rope clotheslines in the breezy autumn sunlight. On Lawndale's West side, children played in dusty vacant lots instead of in landscaped parks like the ones planted along Mary Street.

Naimah, Eddie, Tayesha, Anthony, and Liz went from door to door among the row houses asking people to vote for Shannon Gordon.

"I didn't get out for the referendum vote," confessed one older woman. "I feel bad about that. But I promise you children, Shannon Gordon's going to get my vote this time."

"Thank you," said Naimah. "My mom needs your vote and your support."

At the end of the row houses sat a city block of dilapidated, two-story apartment houses. As they approached one gray apartment building, a grandfatherly-looking man walked stiffly out of the first floor apartment balancing himself with a wooden cane.

"Good afternoon, children," greeted the

grandfather as he sat down carefully on a front porch stool.

"Good afternoon," they replied in unison. Naimah walked up the short flight of steps and handed the man a campaign flyer.

"I hope you don't mind," Naimah began, "but we're out campaigning this afternoon for the re-election of city councilwoman Shannon Gordon."

"Mind?" laughed the grandfather. "Why I've voted for Shannon Gordon every time she's run for office. I voted for Shannon Gordon's plan for redistricting, too," he added, studying Naimah's face. "You seem surprised."

"Well," said Naimah, "I've talked to a lot of people today. Most of them younger than you. People who can get up and get around, but who missed the referendum vote and missed voting in past city council elections, too."

The old man let out a short laugh. "Well," he paused, "maybe some of those young folks don't know what I know. Or maybe they don't remember what black folks went through to get to vote in the first place. It's mighty hard," he said, "to set here at home on election day when you realize that a lot of people died to help us win the right to vote."

The five teens nodded in agreement with the man.

"You make me wish that I was old enough to vote," said Tayesha.

"Me, too," added Liz.

"We could sure use you to help inspire our campaign," said Anthony.

"We sure could," said Liz, Naimah, Tayesha, and Eddie in unison. "We sure could, yeah . . ."

"I'm a little too old for campaigning," sighed the grandfather. "But I can give you a little bit of good advice, though." The old man picked up his cane and pointed to a brownstone tenement building right across the street from where they were standing. "Go across the street over there," he suggested, "and leave some flyers at that shelter for the homeless. Gotta be at least a hundred votes up in there."

Naimah thanked the grandfather and then she, Eddie, Anthony, Tayesha, and Liz walked across the street and entered the shelter. Once inside, the director of the shelter gave them permission to post as many flyers as they wished. Not one of them had ever been inside a shelter before. They were surprised to see that there were so many children. Toys and mattresses without frames were neatly stacked against the walls.

Naimah stepped inside a well-lit, but empty room where she found an open notebook, a math book, pens, and pencils spread across the top of a long wooden folding table. She picked up the math book and from the inside cover discovered the book was the property of DuSable Junior High. She found it hard to believe there were DuSable students living in a homeless shelter. Naimah put a campaign flyer between the pages of the math book and then she left the room.

It was nearing dinner time. Tayesha, Liz, Eddie, and Anthony were waiting for Naimah in the lobby. Naimah went to the director's office to say thanks for letting them distribute flyers. On her way into the office, Naimah ran into a boy about her age.

"Sorry," the boy mumbled. Naimah thought she recognized the boy as she passed by him again on her way to the lobby.

The five friends left the shelter strolling in the afterglow of the autumn afternoon. As they walked home Naimah didn't mention the boy to anyone, but she was certain that she knew the boy she'd bumped into. It was Le Cao Tho, a classmate of hers at school.

CHAPTER FIVE

It took four days for Naimah and her friends to canvas the East, West, North, and South sides of Lawndale. In the passing of those four days, the whole Gordon house had been thrown into a frenzy. Naimah's mother's campaign was in full swing, too. The frenzy seemed to have started in Naimah's room, and from there it spread all through the house like a brush fire. There were flyers, posters, and campaign buttons strewn about the living room. The telephone was constantly ringing and there were volunteers all over the house. Shannon Gordon was busy with door-to-door campaigning. Mr. Gordon was campaign manager and so that left Naimah to fend for herself and the human pest.

Naimah, Liz, Tayesha, Anthony, and Eddie had handed out so many campaign flyers the last week, they were tired of looking at them. Naimah overheard her mother ask her father about the flyers she had seen at different places in the ward. Ms. Gordon knew the flyers weren't from her campaign committee. Naimah's father had said it was probably some organization that wanted to support the campaign on its own.

It was Saturday morning. But with only a few days left to campaign for the student council elections, and only one week left to campaign for her mother, Naimah was used to being up and dressed. She had gotten up early, but not early enough to catch her mother who had already left to go campaigning at the mall.

She ran downstairs to the kitchen where she put on a pot of coffee for her father and the endless stream of volunteers who would soon be pouring into the house. Then she quickly ate a bowl of cold cereal.

Today, phase two of the private campaign would begin. Today and tomorrow, she, Anthony, and Tayesha planned to canvas the new neighborhoods that had been added to the third ward through David Russell's map. Just as she was about to call Anthony and Tayesha, little Rodney walked into the kitchen, rubbing the sleep from his eyes.

"*Uhhmmm*—what smells so good?" yawned the eight-year old. He climbed up on the stool near the counter.

"What smells so good?" mimicked his sister as she placed her bowl and spoon with a clatter into the kitchen sink. Naimah turned facing her brother. With her hands on her hips she replied, *"Kellogg's Cornflakes*, that's what."

"Mom said you're supposed to cook breakfast," Rodney protested. He looked around the kitchen. There were no pots on the stove. No delicious-smelling bacon frying in the pan. There was only the aroma of coffee brewing, which he knew was for grown-ups.

"Mom said—"

"Listen you little—" Naimah stopped herself. "I don't know if you've noticed but we're in the middle of a campaign around here. Nobody's got time to scramble eggs or butter toast for the little prince. If I can eat cereal, you can eat cereal, and that's that!"

Rodney slid off the stool. Wearing a look of hungry disappointment on his face he pouted, "I'm telling Dad." Then he pushed through the swinging door that led out of the kitchen.

A few moments later Mr. Gordon appeared in the kitchen. He was barely awake. He scratched his head, poured himself a cup of coffee, and looked at Naimah.

"Would you please cook your brother some

breakfast? I've got to shower and get on the phone to the volunteers."

"Daddy—"

"Please, Naimah?" Her father cut her short. Then he went upstairs with the mug of coffee in his hand. Naimah scrunched her nose up at her brother but that didn't seem to bother Rodney. He climbed upon a stool and waited patiently for his breakfast. As Naimah cooked, she thought to herself, a little tobasco in his scrambled eggs wouldn't hurt him a bit.

Sunlight gleamed across the spotless Gordon kitchen. Outside the open window, a couple of blue jays were competing in a tournament of raucous squawking. After she cleaned the kitchen, Naimah called Anthony and Tayesha. The trio decided to meet at her house. Next week, phase three of their private campaign would begin. That's when all five of them planned to leaflet the local junior high and high schools.

After Anthony and Tayesha arrived, the three teenagers left Naimah's house and headed towards the park.

As Naimah, Tayesha, and Anthony neared Division Street, they heard a loud speaker blaring out campaign messages. They could see a caravan of cars a short distance away.

"My name is David Russell, and I'm

running for city councilman of the third ward. I'm campaigning for truth, honesty, and integrity in government. I'm campaigning against political deals made in smoke-filled rooms. Please join us with your friends and families in Washington Park for free pizza and ice cream. My name is David Russell. . . ."

The three walked closer to the curb so that they could get a better look. There were three convertible cars with their tops down. The cars were filled with flag-waving supporters of David Russell. Seven or eight junior-and senior-high school students walked beside the cars.

"Hey, look!" exclaimed Anthony, pointing to three boys passing out David Russell campaign flyers. "Isn't that Pete Russell, Hank Rodriguez, and Bill English?"

Naimah stood on her tiptoes so she could see over the crowd that had gathered in front of her.

"Yeah. It is," she said. "What do you suppose Pete and Hank are doing hanging out with Bill?"

Bill English was captain of the DuSable football team. He was a fourteen-year-old mass of muscle with the I.Q. of a donut. Bill was always in the principal's office, getting into trouble for doing stupid things like pulling the fire alarm, or leaving school through emergency-only exits. Pete on the other hand, was an exact clone of his old man. Pete didn't associate with the African-American students at DuSable. And you couldn't trust him or his father as far as you could throw them. Bill English was carrying a brown paper bag filled to the top with something that seemed awfully precious to him. He was moving as though he were walking on eggs. "I smell a rat," said Anthony.

"Yeah, me too." said Naimah

"That makes three," agreed Tayesha.

"Let's go over to the park," Naimah suggested.

Washington Park was like a three-ring circus. There were clowns giving balloons away to small children. There were marching bands, pony rides, a concession stand with free food, and free David Russell posters. Beside the concession stand was a wooden platform from which David Russell was planning to speak. As they neared the concession stand Anthony asked if Tayesha and Naimah wanted something to drink.

"Not me," said Naimah as she walked quickly past the stand.

"On second thought," said Anthony as he picked up speed, "I think I'd rather have a cool drink of water myself."

David Russell was just beginning to deliver his speech. Naimah, Tayesha, and Anthony moved closer to the platform where he was standing. Naimah noticed for the first time just how odd-looking-a-man David Russell was. He was tall, skinny, and had a balding red head with a thin spray of hair that stood on edge like a rooster's comb. He also had an Adam's apple that danced up and down his throat when he spoke. When they reached the edge of the crowd the three friends stopped. As they stood and waited for the speech to begin, Anthony spotted Bill English clowning around with other jocks from DuSable. The jocks busied themselves by tossing eggs to each other.

"Good afternoon. My name is David Russell and I hope you'll vote for me on election day for city councilman of the third ward. It's a pleasure to be here this afternoon to talk to you about the election. As a candidate seeking to represent you, let me first say that I stand for honesty, above all else—integrity and truth in government. My opponent is Shannon Gordon. I don't have to tell you what a negative impact she has had on the ward *and* city."

"That big mouth!" shouted Anthony. He couldn't stand to hear Russell talk about Naimah's mother that way. Impulsively, Anthony pulled a Shannon Gordon campaign leaflet from his backpack and held it up.

"Vote for Shannon Gordon!" he yelled. "Vote for Shannon Gordon!" Then Tayesha and Naimah joined in.

**"VOTE FOR SHANNON GORDON!
VOTE FOR SHANNON GORDON!"**

Suddenly, a hand reached over and ripped the leaflet from Anthony.

"What's going on?" asked Tayesha nervously.

"I don't know," replied Naimah. "Looks like—"

SPLAATT! From out of no where a raw egg hit Naimah in the face and then—**SPLAATT!** Another caught Tayesha in the back of the head. People started pushing each other. Soon there were people shoving and pushing and running all over the place. It was like a minor riot.

Naimah, Anthony, and Tayesha could barely see, but they could hear the people running frantically and tripping over each other. The park was now a scene of mass confusion. Someone knocked Tayesha to the ground. Anthony tried to help her up, but he was knocked down, too. Soon, Naimah was lying beside them. They could see feet and legs all around them, but they couldn't get up.

"Cover your face!" Anthony shouted to Tayesha and Naimah.

"Cover your face!"

A foot came down on the back of Tayesha's leg and she let out a scream. Then, from out of no where two big strong hands helped Tayesha up from the ground. The grass underfoot was slippery with broken eggs, which made standing up nearly impossible. Two strong pair of hands helped Anthony and Naimah up, too. The three friends dusted themselves off.

"Are you all right?" Anthony asked Naimah and Tayesha.

"I guess so," Tayesha answered rubbing her leg.

And then a loud voice boomed, "You're going to the police station! All three of you." It was one of the men with strong hands. They were policemen. But neither Naimah, Tayesha, or Anthony had noticed—at first.

"That's right, officer!" yelled someone from the crowd. "They started it."

"We didn't start anything," protested

Naimah.

"You'd better come with us," demanded the police officer.

"What did we do?" Anthony asked nervously.

"Just come with us. Let's go!"

The Gordons, the Williames, and Ms. Young stood in the lobby of the police station as their children were being led from the back. No one said a word. All of the parents were either angry, disappointed, or both.

When Naimah got into the car, her mother slammed the door so hard behind her, Naimah thought it was going to fall off. Naimah knew her mother was very angry because she didn't say anything for a long time. Even her dad didn't say anything. Finally, Ms. Gordon spoke.

"Naimah, didn't I tell you to let me handle David Russell? Now look at what's happened. The election is right around the corner. This episode can only hurt the campaign."

Naimah sat sullenly in the back seat of the car. Rodney was trying hard not to crack up laughing. He tried to maintain his cool by looking out the car window.

"I can't understand why you would go over to the park in the first place," continued Ms. Gordon. "You must have known it was a rally for

David Russell.

"Mom," Naimah tried to explain, "I was out delivering flyers for your campaign."

"At Washington Park? Where David Russell was delivering a campaign speech? You know the kind of supporters he has. And who gave you permission to hand out flyers in the first place?"

"Mama, I didn't do anything wrong," Naimah said plaintively. "None of us did. Me and Anthony and Tayesha didn't start anything. Somebody threw eggs at us."

"Naimah, I asked you to help your father out at home. There are a million things you could do at home to help my campaign. I should have known something was going on. You're the one who has been passing out all those flyers, aren't you?" Naimah didn't answer.

"Don't you hear me talking to you Naimah Zakia Jackson?!"

"Yes. Me, Tayesha, Liz, Anthony, and Eddie passed them out," Naimah answered softly.

Naimah's mother looked out the car window and stared at the soft lights shining from the bungalows along Mary Street. Naimah looked down at her brother. He was rocking back and forth, holding his mouth and stomach. He was trying hard to keep from laughing out loud. He succeeded in holding the laughter in, but the strain made tears stream down his face.

"Well, young lady—" sighed Shannon Gordon, "No more campaigning for you. You're grounded for a week." Naimah scooted down in the back seat of the car and let her eyes roam over the solemn brick houses as they slid past the car window.

Finally, they reached their driveway. Once inside the house Naimah turned to her mother. "Mom—" she began.

"Not now, Naimah," said Shannon Gordon. "You go on upstairs to your room. We'll talk about it later." Rodney darted past his sister and raced up the steps. When he reached the top he turned around and whispered in a hoarse laugh— "See ya! And I wouldn't want to be ya!"

He ran to his room almost dying from laughter.

CHAPTER SIX

It was Monday, and with the city council election now just one week away, Naimah was still grounded. Forbidden to work on her mother's campaign, she focused on her own student council school election. Over the weekend she busied herself making campaign posters. And bright and early Monday morning Tayesha, Eddie, Liz, and Anthony had met her at school and helped her put them up around campus.

Tomorrow was the big day. . .the day of the school election. A big assembly was planned with cheerleaders and the school's marching band, too.

Eddie and Naimah were spending their lunch hour putting up the last posters before the election tomorrow.

"Let's put this one outside the gym," Eddie suggested. Just as they finished taping the poster near the gym door, Bill English burst through the doors almost knocking the two of them down.

"Hey, man!" said Eddie. "You got a problem or something?"

Bill English sucked in his stomach and pumped up his chest. He had spiked hair and wore a gold earring in his left ear.

"I think you've got the problem, little man," said Bill. He grinned and clenched his big fists. Naimah quickly stepped in between the two of them.

"Forget it, Eddie," pleaded Naimah. "There's been enough trouble already."

"Yeah, Eddie," laughed Bill. "You guys are already walking on hot coals."

Eddie started toward Bill. Naimah grabbed his arm and held him back. Bill walked away laughing.

"Dumb, jock!" shouted Eddie after him. Bill turned and waved his hand as though Eddie were a fly he was shooing away.

"Catch an egg, Eddie," he shouted and laughed.

"So, you're the one who threw those eggs! You'll get yours, man!" Eddie shouted again. "You're going to get yours."

"Don't pay him any attention, Eddie," Naimah said calmly. "That's exactly what he wants. Guys like Bill, Pete, and David Russell don't care about other people. So they do stupid things and say stupid things to start trouble."

"It's not fair and it stinks," replied Eddie.

"You're right," Naimah agreed. "It does stink. But if we keep plugging away, maybe we can make a difference in spite of people like them."

"I hope you're right," said Eddie.

"Come on," said Naimah. She picked up the posters from the floor.

"We've only got ten minutes left. Let's grab something to eat before the bell rings."

After school Naimah found Liz, Anthony, Eddie, and Tayesha waiting for her on the bleachers. Liz was wearing a pair of red-rimmed sunglasses, a brocade vest, and a black, silk top hat.

"You really look sharp," Naimah said to her.

"Tonight's the big night," said Liz excitedly. "I made it through the auditions. This is the big one. I hope you guys will be there."

"Not me," said Naimah disappointedly. "I'm grounded. Remember?"

"Thank God I'm not grounded anymore," Tayesha said.

"Well, I'm just glad the police didn't charge us," said Anthony. "They could have if they'd wanted to. We could've really gotten into trouble."

"Yeah," said Naimah. "They definitely could have—even though we didn't really do anything wrong. If I hadn't suggested going to the park in the first place none of this would have happened."

"But you were doing what you thought was the right thing," remarked Liz.

"Yeah, and look at the trouble it got me into," replied Naimah.

"It was really all my fault," admitted Anthony. "I shouldn't have lost my cool."

Liz glanced at her watch. "I really have to go," she said as she leaped to her feet. "All the contestants have to be backstage no later than six o'clock."

"I'll be there, Liz," said Tayesha smiling.

"Eddie and I are getting a ride from his mom," said Anthony.

"Don't worry," said Eddie. "We'll be there. We won't let you down."

"Thanks a million, guys," said Liz. She waved good-bye and dashed across the school grounds.

"Break a leg, girlfriend!" shouted Naimah. "Break a leg!"

"Now, there you go with that girlfriend stuff," protested Eddie. "I hate that."

"Don't be so uptight, Eddie. Relax," advised Anthony.

Naimah looked at the time. It was almost three-fifteen. "I have to go," she said. "I have to be home by three-thirty or else." She hurried across the school yard. Eddie, Anthony, and Tayesha followed her.

The next day at school everyone was congratulating Liz.

"Great job, Liz!"

"Do it, homegirl!"

"Way to go!"

Liz was busy blowing kisses to her new fan club. As far as she was concerned she was still on stage.

"You could at least be a little modest," Tayesha joked as they neared school.

"Why should I? I'm a star."

"Aw, girl."

"Well, I am. The next stop is Los Angeles, California. When I get my contract, I'll be hanging out with Bel Biv DeVoe. Tevin Campbell. Boyz II Men, Mariah Carey."

"Stop it, girl."

"You were great, Liz!" someone yelled from across the street.

"Thank you," said Liz, taking a deep bow and fluttering her eyelashes. She was trying hard to act like a star.

"You don't know how truly excited I am, dear." She turned and smiled at Tayesha.

"You're too much, Liz." Tayesha had to smile, too. The two girls walked to the bleachers. There were ten minutes left before the first bell. Liz sat down on one of the benches. In no time at all she was surrounded by wannabees and well-wishers. Decked out in a gold-sequined pants suit, a pair of black, knee-high boots, a black beret, and one gold dangling earring she really did look like a star.

Tayesha just sat there watching her friend bask in her glory. Suddenly, Liz saw Naimah approaching. She almost lost her cool. She and Tayesha rushed to greet Naimah.

"I told you I would do it!" she said excitedly.

"Congratulations, girl," smiled Naimah. She gave Liz a big hug.

"I blew them away, didn't I, Tayesha?! You should have been there, girlfriend."

"I wish I could have," said Naimah. "But there will be other times. So now, where's the color television set?"

"In front of the waterbed, girlfriend," Liz answered smiling.

"And the gift certificates?"

"Ready to be spent." The three girls laughed.

"You ready for your campaign speech?" Liz asked Naimah, changing the subject.

"As ready as I'll ever be," said Naimah.

"I've had a lot of time to practice."

"When you get on that stage, keep your eye on me," Liz instructed. "I'll be easy to spot. I'll be the one clapping the loudest."

"Next to me that is," added Tayesha.

The bell rang and Naimah, Liz, and Tayesha headed for the school building.

The ten o'clock assembly was noisy and loud. Mr. Maloney, the school principal introduced the candidates for president of the DuSable Junior High student council. Each had to make a speech. Pete Russell was first.

"Good morning. My name is Pete Russell, and I hope you'll vote for me for president of student council. It's a pleasure to be here this morning to talk to you about DuSable Junior High School and the election. As a candidate seeking to represent you, let me first say that I stand for honesty, integrity, and truth in student government. . . ."

Naimah groaned and slid down in her chair. She recognized the words in the speech Pete was giving. It was the same speech his father delivered at the Washington Park rally. Pete Russell was such a phony. He couldn't deliver his own speech, Naimah thought.

"I urge you to think about what has happened to DuSable the last few years. Think about how much our school has changed. DuSable used to be an all white school. Look around you. DuSable is majority black now. The African-American students are taking over DuSable."

Some of the white students rose and began to applaud, but more than half the auditorium began to boo. Mr. Maloney had to get up and stand in front of the stage.

He's just like his father, thought Naimah. I bet he thinks all the white students are going to vote for him just because he's white.

The rest of Russell's talk, sprinkled with promises of better vending machines, more dances, and better uniforms for the football and baseball teams, was delivered in such a boring monotone it nearly lulled the entire assembly hall to sleep.

"And so, as you cast your vote this afternoon, cast your vote for a change. Vote for me, Pete Russell, for president of the DuSable student council."

Mr. Maloney, the principal, tried to alert the rest of the audience that Pete had finished his speech by walking up and down the aisles briskly, clapping his hands like a large seal. But the students didn't have a clue as to what was going on. Then suddenly the band woke from its slumber and blasted out a fighting march song, causing the audience of seventh and eighth graders to respond with an obligatory applause. Some of the white students applauded loudly for Pete. They tried in vain to get other students to applaud.

"We want Pete. . . .We want Pete. . . ."

But the spark for Pete Russell was barely ignited before the next candidate for student council, Henry Garcia Rodriguez took the podium.

The audience's response to Hank Rodriguez was a little more enthusiastic than it had been for Pete. Hank was smart and he was well-liked. But all of Hank's campaign promises seemed to be directed towards the Latino students.

"Other schools have soccer teams. Why can't we have one?"

A groundswell of applause rose from three adjoining sections of the assembly. The band blasted out a few bars of a march.

"Other schools study Latin-American history. Why can't we study Latin-American history? DuSable needs more Latino counselors and more Latino teachers."

More applause ascended from the Hank Rodriguez section of the assembly. Hank's speech lasted for ten more minutes. After he finished, the band struck up another march and the cheerleaders did cartwheels across the stage. Finally, it was Naimah's turn to speak.

By now the audience of seventh and eighth graders was fidgety and bored. During her opponents' speeches, snickers could be heard coming from some of the students. Mr. Maloney stood up in front of the auditorium. The one spotlight lighting the stage cast quite a glare on his balding head. Mr. Maloney folded his arms across his chest and peered over his spectacles. The noise quickly subsided.

Ms. Fuller, the Vice Principal, went to the microphone.

"And now, for our last candidate for the office of president of student council—let's give a round of applause to Naimah Jackson."

Suddenly, the auditorium seemed to come to life. The band stood up and began playing and marching in place. The cheerleaders tossed aside their pom poms, left the stage, and somersaulted up and down the assembly hall aisles.

Naimah felt nervous. She looked for her four friends. She spotted Liz clapping her hands vigorously. Then she saw Tayesha and Anthony standing in the front row.

"**NAIMAH! NAIMAH! NAIMAH!**" they shouted.

Eddie stood next to Tayesha and Anthony. He whistled boldly through his fingers right in front of Mr. Maloney. The momentum began to spread from row to row until finally half the auditorium was standing and shouting: "**NAIMAH! NAIMAH! NAIMAH!**"

Ms. Fuller motioned for Naimah to start her speech. Naimah walked slowly to the microphone.

"Thank you! Thank you!" she said. "Thank you!"

Now it was quiet.

"Today I come before you, the student body of DuSable Junior High School, to ask that you vote for me for president of the student council. I ask you to vote for me to help me make DuSable an even better school. . . ."

As Naimah spoke the students really seemed to listen.

". . . .When you vote today, vote for the

best candidate," said Naimah. "Vote for the best candidate—and not for the color of the candidate's skin. Vote for leadership. Vote for the right to have a voice in what goes on in your school. DuSable is a good school, but it could be better. We do need more minority teachers . . . African-American, Latino, and Asian. We need a better lunchroom and more after-school activities. Not just sports—everybody at DuSable *isn't* an athlete."

A huge wave of applause rose from all over the assembly hall.

"We *need* peer counseling. Students ought to have a place where they can sit and talk with kids their own age. DuSable is the only junior high in the area that doesn't have peer counseling. As students, we need to take more responsibility for what goes on both inside and outside our school. Some of our students are homeless. They leave DuSable every day and go home to shelters. As their classmates, we have a responsibility to reach out and try to support them."

The students applauded loudly again, especially Le Cao Tho, who was now on his feet.

That afternoon, Naimah won the election.

After school, she met her friends by the bleachers.

"Way to go, Madam President," teased Eddie.

"Yeah, Naimah," agreed Anthony, "You really gave a great speech. Your mom couldn't have done better."

"Hey!" said Eddie, suddenly jumping down from the bleachers. "Why don't we celebrate? Liz is going to be rich and famous some day. She just won a big talent show. And Naimah's going to be President of the United States. C'mon," said Eddie. "What're we waiting for?"

"I'm still grounded, Eddie," said Naimah sounding exasperated.

"Well, let's at least give three cheers for Mary Street," shouted Eddie. "This is a day to remember."

Then Eddie threw his cap into the air—as high as he could.

CHAPTER SEVEN

Several days had passed since Naimah had been grounded. Coming straight home from school had already become routine. Once the student council campaign had ended, the rest of the week seemed to drag by slowly. Today was only Thursday. Naimah went home and started her homework. She struggled through the twenty-five algebra equations Mr. Fermoyle had assigned. Even though she always made the honor roll each quarter, math was not one of her favorite subjects. She was a wiz at history and English, but math was another story.

She finished the last equation. As she pushed away from her desk she heard a knock on the door. It was her mother.

"Hi," Ms. Gordon said. "Got a minute for the old lady?"

"Sure, Mom. Come on in."

Shannon Gordon came in and sat down on the bed across from her daughter.

"How was school today?"

"Too much work as usual." Naimah answered with a little smile.

As Ms. Gordon looked at her daughter, she realized how much Robert Jackson, Naimah's real dad, lived in her young face. Naimah might've looked more like her at first glance, but she had her father's cheekbones and chin. Robert Jackson had been a writer, but he had died before achieving success.

"I've got a lot of algebra equations to do this week," Naimah went on. "But other than that, I guess I'll survive eighth grade."

"You didn't tell me about the election at school."

"You were real busy, Mom," answered Naimah.

Ms. Gordon sighed.

"I guess I have been busy. But I want you to know that I'm very proud of you. I heard about your speech. Some people think you're ready for the big time."

Naimah blushed.

"Not really."

Ms. Gordon smiled at Naimah and ran her hand over her hair.

"Your father would have been proud of you. Yes, I'm certain he would have been. We're all proud of you—Rodney, your stepdad, *and* me."

"It's just a student election."

"I'm sure the students you defeated wouldn't say that."

Naimah smiled.

"I guess they wouldn't," she agreed.

Ms. Gordon stood up. For one of the few times, she seemed to be searching for words.

"I guess I have been rough on you lately, huh? Well, I guess I have been a little rough on everybody. I want you to know that I realize that when you were taken to the police station, you were just trying to help. It wasn't a smart move, but I know you were trying to help my campaign. I guess I overreacted. Maybe I shouldn't have grounded you."

"I did something stupid. It could have been used against you, and I could've been hurt."

"Yes, you could have been. But you didn't plan it that way. I just want you to know that I appreciate your concern for me. When this election is over, maybe we all can go away for a weekend. We sure need it."

Shannon Gordon put her hand on her daughter's shoulder and squeezed it firmly.

"Still love me?"

"I'll always love you, Mom."

"I love you too, honey." She smiled again at her daughter and then Shannon Gordon left the room.

CHAPTER EIGHT

Naimah awoke to the smell of bacon, floating up from the kitchen. It was Sunday morning. Only two days left before city council elections. She'd slept late and awakened hungry. So she took a quick shower, dressed, and went down to breakfast.

As usual, little Rodney was half stuffed before anybody else had even fixed themselves a plate. Her mom and dad were nursing coffee mugs filled with piping hot coffee and studying the Sunday paper.

"Good morning," yawned Naimah, helping herself to a plate of bacon, scrambled eggs, and french toast.

"Hi, honey," answered her mother without taking her eyes off the newspaper.

"Morning, Naimah," said Mr. Gordon. He was scanning the headlines with a frown.

"How're the polls looking?" Naimah asked as she took a bite from the french toast.

Shannon Gordon sighed heavily. She had a look on her face that said "bad, really bad."

"Not too good," she said lifting her coffee mug to her mouth. Naimah watched her mom's worried expression.

"We're seven points behind and there're only a couple of days left," Mr. Gordon said.

"If only the court had decided to hear the redistricting case before the election," Ms. Gordon added dejectedly.

"What good would the hearing do after the election?" asked Naimah.

"Well, the court could reverse Russell's redistricting victory. But it would have saved a lot of trouble and money if the case had been heard before the election. Well, as they say, 'when handed a lemon, make lemonade,'" said Shannon Gordon getting up from the table.

All of a sudden Naimah lost her appetite. She knew her mother was the best candidate. But she also knew that her mother's chances of winning the election at seven points behind in the polls were not very good.

"I'm running late," said Shannon Gordon as she kissed her husband and children on her way out of the kitchen. Before leaving, she gave her husband some last minute details.

"Break a leg, Mom," shouted Rodney.

"Yeah, break a leg." Naimah had to struggle to get the words out. Shannon Gordon was off to continue her campaign.

As soon as her mother left Naimah called Anthony.

"I was sort of expecting a call from you," Anthony said.

"Listen up," said Naimah, "Can you come over?"

"Yeah. On the way, I'll stop by Eddie's and bring him over, too."

Volunteers began filling the house. Soon, there were volunteers everywhere. By the time Tayesha, Eddie, Anthony, and Liz arrived, there was no place for them to meet except in Naimah's bedroom.

"My mom is seven points behind in the polls," Naimah explained.

"Not good," said Eddie.

"We don't have much time left," observed Tayesha.

"What're we going to do?" asked Liz.

Naimah toyed nervously with the charm bracelet she had put on her wrist earlier in the day.

"Let's call a rally," Naimah said suddenly. "We could invite every junior and senior high school in the ward. We've got to let the students know how important this election is."

"If we can get students to put pressure on their parents, maybe we can get more people to vote." added Anthony.

"And to support Ms. Gordon's re-election," said Tayesha.

"Naimah," Liz jumped in. "Sandy's running for student council president at her school. She supports your mom's re-election. Let's get her to speak at the rally."

"That would be great!" Naimah exclaimed. "Who's her running mate?"

"Marita Perez," answered Liz.

"See if you can get Marita to speak at the rally, too."

"Bet," said Liz.

"Anthony, doesn't your cousin hold a council seat at Crane High School?" Naimah asked.

"For two years straight," Anthony smiled proudly.

"Think you can get him to come to the rally?"

"No problem," he assured Naimah.

"Tayesha," asked Naimah, "can you get over to Lincoln Junior High tomorrow before school and round up their student council leaders?"

"I'll try," answered Tayesha.

"Invite all of them," said Naimah.

"And Eddie—see if you can contact the officers from Marshall High School."

"Done. What day and what time are we looking at?"

"Monday," answered Naimah. "Monday afternoon at four o'clock in Garfield Park."

"Right after school?" Anthony asked, "This is going to be difficult." Naimah looked Anthony right in the eyes.

"We don't have a choice."

CHAPTER NINE

Naimah, Liz, Anthony, Tayesha, and Eddie spent all of Sunday afternoon painting banners and posters that announced the upcoming rally. Early Monday morning they distributed the flyers and put the posters up at strategic locations.

By three forty-five on Monday afternoon, Garfield Park was swarming with junior-and senior-high school students. Naimah, Tayesha, Liz, Anthony, and Eddie huddled near the park bleachers. As they looked around the park, they could see that their hard work had paid off. There were hundreds and hundreds of students. There were African-American students, Caucasian students, Latino students, and Asian students.

Television minivans, camera persons, and reporters were there, too. Reporters were interviewing students randomly, trying to find out exactly what was going on.

All the students gathered near the bleachers.

"Well, Naimah," Eddie said, "it's your mom, so it's your show."

Naimah walked to the top of the park bleachers. She held a bullhorn in her hand and looked out at the sea of students. She swallowed hard and then held the bullhorn up to her mouth.

"PARENTS MUST VOTE! PARENTS MUST VOTE!" she chanted.

The crowd of teenagers picked up Naimah's chant, and soon adults, walking along the streets bordering the park, began to gather.

As the chant died down, Naimah shouted out at the crowd.

"Tomorrow is a very important day in our city. It's the day that those people who represent us in government will be elected! We're too young to vote! But we're not too young to urge our parents to vote! **PARENTS MUST VOTE!**"

The crowd of students once again picked up Naimah's chant:

"PARENTS MUST VOTE! PARENTS MUST VOTE! PARENTS MUST VOTE! PARENTS MUST VOTE!"

"Look around you." Naimah continued.

"This is our city, not just our parents' city! It's our future we're talking about, not just the future of our parents! Sure, we're too young to vote! But that doesn't mean we can't be concerned about our city and the people who run it!"

A cheer rose from the crowd.

"In the third ward, where we live, a new map has been drawn, adding new voters. Some of the new voters are white. One of the candidates running for office in the third ward is an African American. That candidate is my mother, city councilwoman Shannon Gordon." Again the crowd applauded loud and vigorously.

"For the last eight years, councilwoman Gordon has worked very hard for the people of the third ward and for the people of our city. She deserves to keep her office. She is a better leader than her opponent could ever be. Tonight, when you go home, remind your parents that there are decent, hardworking candidates running for office who deserve their support. Ask your parents to take a good look at Shannon Gordon's record, and urge them to vote for the best candidate. Tell them not to vote for the color of the candidate's skin. Tell them to vote for the candidate's record."

By the time Naimah finished speaking there were almost as many adults drifting towards the bleachers as students. And the cheering that followed came from both students and adults. After Naimah spoke Marita Perez and Sandy Butler followed.

Marita talked about how she'd helped to register people who could barely speak English, but who were determined to exercise their right to vote.

With the bullhorn in her hand Marita shouted: "Don't let your parents play you off by saying their vote won't matter! You and I both know better! Every vote counts! Talk to your parents! Tell them to make the right choice! That right choice is Shannon Gordon!"

The rally lasted for nearly an hour. More than twenty students spoke.

It wasn't long before the television reporters and newspaper reporters figured out that Naimah was the leader of the rally. They began trailing her. But somehow Naimah managed to keep them at bay. She didn't want her mother to find out that she was the leader of the rally. She didn't know what her mother would say. And sometimes, it's better to be safe than sorry, she thought.

After the rally was over, Naimah and her supporters stayed behind to clean up the discarded flyers, posters, and paper.

As Naimah picked up a pair of discarded sneakers, she overheard a television reporter taping his news report.

"Never before has such an ethnically diverse group of young people turned out to support so serious an issue. There was no chaos. No trouble whatsoever. It certainly was not like some of the rock and rap concerts we've been hearing about," the reporter said.

"There is speculation that this rally just might do what it was intended to do. . . help Shannon Jackson Gordon's sagging re-election bid. The two-time councilwoman has needed a boost ever since her redistricting plan lost to former policeman David Russell's plan. Russell is her opponent in this race and, according to polls conducted yesterday, he has a substantial lead. But it looks like this inspiring rally is going to change that.

This is Paul Snyder reporting for Channel 3 News."

Shannon Gordon sat in her living room watching the Channel 3 News. She was surrounded by volunteer campaign workers. She glanced at her watch and wondered where Naimah was.

Naimah can't have anything to do with this, she thought. Or could she? Shannon Gordon smiled, because she knew the answer.

CHAPTER TEN

On election night, Mary Street was buzzing with activities. Cars were double parked. A crowd had gathered on the lawn of the Gordon's house. A steady flow of campaign volunteers, neighbors, and friends came and went. The sun had set and the lights had begun to brighten the street and the houses.

Inside the Gordon house, a festive, confident air prevailed. There was music softly playing. The walls were dotted with colorful balloons and streamers and the smell of fried chicken, collard greens, and smothered pepper steak with rice beckoned the crowd towards the kitchen.

In the living room, Shannon and Rodney Gordon were surrounded by volunteers huddled around the television. The recent precinct reports were good. Earlier in the day, news reports indicated that Shannon Gordon had closed the gap on David Russell. It was an even race the reports said. The reports also predicted a significant number of white voters would turn out for Shannon Gordon. Early reports showed the race to be neck and neck. But returns had not come in from the section of the ward where Ms. Gordon had the greatest support.

"Looking good, Shannon," shouted Anthony's mother over the noise of the growing crowd. Shannon looked up from the television and raised a victorious fist in the air.

"Keep your fingers crossed, Pat," said Ms. Gordon, crossing her own two fingers as an example.

"It's already over," announced Floyd Delaney. "You've got it won, Shannon."

"You know what they say," Henry Williams interjected.

"It's not over 'til the fat lady sings," his wife answered.

"The fat lady is all out of breath, now," Mr. Delaney said laughing. "I tell you, this election is over."

"Let's be sure," Juanita Delaney told her husband.

"All right. Nobody wants to listen to me. I tell you, I've been watching these elections long enough to know."

"Why don't you all go in the kitchen and get

something to eat," Ms. Gordon said to the Delaneys, Williamses, Youngs, Butlers, and other well wishers who had not eaten.

"There's plenty to eat," said Mr. Gordon.

"I think I will," Mr. Delaney said. He, Mr. and Ms. Butler, and Henry Williams walked into the kitchen.

Little Rodney busied himself playing hide-and-seek with several neighborhood children. Every few minutes he made pit stops to the kitchen. Naimah, Eddie, Tayesha, Liz, and Anthony were in Naimah's room. Naimah had borrowed the television from her parents room. There were several bowls of snacks, a package of cookies, and soda on top of the dresser.

"Why does it take so long?" Naimah was getting impatient.

"The polls closed at eight," Anthony said. "It takes time to count the votes. But can you imagine what it will mean if your mother beats David Russell even without the help of the court?"

"You bet," smiled Naimah. "It'll mean people did the right thing on their own."

"Can you imagine that?" remarked Liz.

"Shhhhhhhh!" interrupted Tayesha, "More returns are coming in."

The five listened intently to the newscaster. But little had changed.

"Man, it's going to take forever," Eddie protested. "I'm going to fall asleep. I've got football practice tomorrow."

"Hey, listen, you guys," Naimah said, "I want to thank you all for helping me out. The campaign and rally wouldn't have been a success without you. Thanks a lot."

"Mush. Mush," joked Eddie. "Bring out the handkerchief." Naimah gave him a playful punch.

Just then, new numbers flashed on the board on the television.

Look!" shouted Anthony. "More votes have come in."

"I think we have a prediction in the third ward," the news reporter announced.

"Turn it up!" yelled Tayesha. Eddie turned up the volume.

"Based upon returns we have so far, it looks like city councilwoman Shannon Jackson Gordon has retained her seat. Again, we predict that Shannon Gordon, of the third ward, will retain her seat with about 58% of the vote. More than seventy-five percent of the vote is in, and we feel certain our prediction will hold."

Pure bedlam, joy, and excitement broke out

inside the Gordon house. People were blowing party horns and shouting congratulations. Some were even tossing confetti around. When the news reached those standing out front, there was laughter followed by shouts of jubilation.

Naimah jumped up and down. She hugged Tayesha. She hugged Liz. She hugged Anthony. She hugged Eddie. She would have hugged Rodney if he were there. Her friends were happy, too. They hugged each other. Eddie and Anthony gave each other high fives and clasped hands. Then Eddie threw his old baseball cap into the air. It hit the ceiling and crashed back to the floor.

"We are bad, y'all," Liz said excitedly.

"Yeah," added Eddie, "We're ready for the big time now."

"You know what?" said Naimah, "we should give ourselves a name."

"I've already thought of that," offered Anthony.

"NEATE," he said. "It's the first letter of each of our first names. N for Naimah. E for Elizabeth. A for Anthony. T for Tayesha and E for Eddie.

"That's fresh," said Liz.

"No, that's NEATE," said Eddie.

"No! *We're* NEATE," joked Tayesha.

The five friends laughed and hugged each other.

Naimah ran out of the room and down the stairs. She wanted to congratulate her mother.

"Mom! Mom!" Naimah yelled as she broke through the circle of well-wishers surrounding her mother.

"Congratulations, Mom! I knew you could do it."

"Something tells me," Ms. Gordon whispered to her daughter, "that a lot of the thanks goes to you."

Ms. Gordon pulled Naimah closer to her.

"You've made me very proud, Naimah."

Suddenly, the little human pest broke through the newly forming circle surrounding his mother and sister. He climbed on the sofa, jumped on his mother's back and locked his arms around her neck.

"Congratulations, Mom!" he said. "We did it! We did it!" Shannon Gordon reached back and hugged her son.

Then the councilwoman embraced her daughter. She and Naimah held each other for a long time.

Tell Us What You Think About NEATE™!

Name _____

Address _____

City _____ State ____ Zip _____

Date of Birth _____

1. Who is your favorite NEATE™ character? _____

2. What kind of story would you like to see NEATE™ take on?
    (a) mystery (b) adventure (c) romance (d) other _____

3. How did you get your first copy of NEATE™?
    (a) parent (b) gift (c) own purchase (d) other _____

4. Are you looking forward to the next title in the NEATE™ series?
    (a) yes (b) no _____
        If no, why? _____
_____
_____

5. Is there anything else you'd like to add? _____
_____
_____
_____
_____

Send your reply to
Editor: NEATE™
    c/o Just Us Books, Inc.
        356 Glenwood Avenue
        East Orange, NJ 07017

MEET

Naimah

Naimah is a proud, self-assured thirteen year old. A born leader, she enjoys coming up with answers to difficult situations. Everyone says she looks just like her mother, who is a member of city council. Naimah loves the comparison. Naimah's mother has remarried and Naimah is fond of her step-dad. But her little brother Rodney, however, is another story. To her, he is the "human-pest."

Elizabeth

Liz just knows she is going to be *the* next pop superstar. She can sing and has won a number of talent shows, but she tends to overdo it a bit. Liz wears leather suits and other flashy garb her father buys for her. One week, her hair is long and flowing. The next week it is in braids. She is always searching for a new style. But, she is a "singer," isn't she?

ANTHONY

Anthony is very bright
and studious. He is
smaller than other kids
his age, and sometimes
that annoys him.
Anthony's mother is a
single parent and he
has never seen his
father. He feels that he
is the man of the house
and must take care of
his mother. She is,
however, very capable
of taking care of herself
and Anthony. Anthony
works hard at every-
thing he does and
wants to be a lawyer
like Eddie's father.

TAYESHA

Tayesha's father is
African American and
her mother is German.
Her parents met when
her father, an army
veteran, was stationed
in Germany. Tayesha is
quite sensitive about
her interracial back-
ground. She has
always been aware of
the stares her family
receives wherever they
go. Quick to stand up
for the underdog,
Tayesha doesn't
understand why some
people can be so mean
and hateful.

EDDIE

Eddie's given name is
Martin Edward De-
laney, but everyone calls
him Eddie. He prefers it
that way. Eddie's father
named him after Dr.
Martin Luther King, Jr.
and never lets him
forget it. "You've got to
have drive and determi-
nation, Eddie, if you
want to succeed. You
can't be lazy." That's
Eddie's father. "Sure,
Dad," Eddie is apt to
respond. Eddie loves
sports, although he is
not really good at any
one of them.

About the Author

Debbi Chocolate is a writer, storyteller, and educator. She received a bachelor's degree from Spelman College in Atlanta, Georgia and a master's degree from Brown University in Providence, Rhode Island. She has worked as an editor, a high school English teacher, and her written work has appeared in a number of national magazines.

Ms. Chocolate is the author of several picture books. They include *Kwanzaa*, published by Children's Press and *My First Kwanza Book* published by Scholastic, Inc. *NEATE™ To the Rescue* is her first published novel for older readers.

OTHER TITLES FROM JUST US BOOKS

AFRO-BETS® Book of Black Heroes From A to Z
by Wade Hudson and Valerie Wilson Wesley

Book of Black Heroes Vol 2:
Great Women in the Struggle ed. by Toyomi Igus

Bright Eyes, Brown Skin by Cheryl Willis Hudson
and Bernette Ford, illustrated by George Ford

Jamal's Busy Day by Wade Hudson, illustrated by
George Ford

When I Was Little by Toyomi Igus, illustrated by
Higgins Bond

Also . . .

AFRO-BETS® A B C Book by Cheryl Willis Hudson

AFRO-BETS® 1 2 3 Book by Cheryl Willis Hudson

AFRO-BETS® Book of Colors by Margery W. Brown

AFRO-BETS® Book of Shapes by Margery W. Brown

AFRO-BETS® First Book About Africa by Veronica Freeman Ellis,
illustrated by George Ford

AFRO-BETS® Activity and Coloring Book by Dwayne Ferguson

AFRO-BETS® Kids: I'm Gonna Be! by Wade Hudson,
illustrated by Culverson Blair

Land of the Four Winds by Veronica Freeman Ellis,
illustrated by Sylvia Walker

Please visit our website for current publications www.justusbooks.com